Harriet

FAT PUSS
FRIENDS
and
FAT PUSS ON
WHEELS

Illustrated by
Colin West

PUFFIN BOOKS

Published by the Penguin Group
Penguin Books Ltd, 27 Wrights Lane, London W8 5TZ, England
Penguin Books USA Inc., 375 Hudson Street, New York, New York 10014, USA
Penguin Books Australia Ltd, Ringwood, Victoria, Australia
Penguin Books Canada Ltd, 10 Alcorn Avenue, Toronto, Ontario, Canada M4V 3B2
Penguin Books (NZ) Ltd, 182–190 Wairau Road, Auckland 10, New Zealand

Penguin Books Ltd, Registered Offices: Harmondsworth, Middlesex, England

Fat Puss and Friends first published by Viking Kestrel 1984
Published in Puffin Books 1985
Fat Puss on Wheels first published by Viking Kestrel 1988
Published in Puffin Books 1989

A Puffin Book exclusively for School Book Fairs 1995
1 3 5 7 9 10 8 6 4 2

Text copyright © Harriet Castor, 1984, 1988
Illustrations copyright © Colin West, 1984, 1988
All rights reserved

Made and printed in England by Clays Ltd, St Ives plc

Harriet Castor

FAT PUSS AND FRIENDS

Illustrated by
Colin West

Another book by Harriet Castor

FAT PUSS AND SLIMPUP

CONTENTS

Fat Puss

Fat Puss was fat. He had little thin
arms, small flat feet, a very short tail
and an amazingly fat tummy.

Fat Puss was sad because all his
friends teased him about being so fat.
He was so enormous that there were
lots of things he couldn't do.

Other cats could squeeze through
holes in fencing.

But Fat Puss couldn't.

Other cats could jump delicately onto thin bars.

But Fat Puss couldn't.

Other cats could walk through cat flaps.

But Fat Puss couldn't.

Other cats could hide in long grass.

But Fat Puss couldn't.

Other cats could walk about silently.
But Fat Puss couldn't.

One day when Fat Puss was feeling particularly sad, he decided to take a walk to cheer himself up. He plodded along, trying to think of something exciting to do.

Then, just as he came to the top of a hill, Fat Puss tripped over a stone!

And he rolled,

and he rolled,

18

and he rolled all the way down the
hill, right to the bottom.

When Fat Puss finally stopped
rolling, he sat up. He had not been
hurt at all. In fact he had rather
enjoyed his unusual form of
travelling.

So when Fat Puss came to the next
hill, he rolled down that too. "Yippee!
This is fun!" he cried.

The next day Fat Puss told all his
friends about his great new pastime.

All Fat Puss's friends tried rolling
down hills, but because they had such
long legs and long tails and were so
thin and bony they couldn't roll
properly and so got very bruised.

"Oh, we wish we could roll down hills like you, Fat Puss," they said.

Then Fat Puss was happy. He didn't mind that the other cats could do things that he couldn't because at last he had found an exciting thing that he and only he could do!

Fat Puss
Finds a Friend

Fat Puss was feeling miserable.
He had been rolling down hills so
much that his tummy was sore. So
he couldn't roll down hills any more
and he had nothing to do.

All Fat Puss's friends were busy chasing mice.

Fat Puss had tried to chase mice too, but he could never catch them because he couldn't run very fast.

Fat Puss felt so miserable that he sat down in a corner and cried.

Just then Fat Puss heard a little
voice.

"Hello," squeaked the little voice.
Fat Puss looked down. There, in front
of him, sat a small mouse. "Hello,"
said the mouse again.

Seeing the mouse made Fat Puss cry even more. All the other cats could have caught it but Fat Puss knew that if he tried to catch the mouse it would just run away so fast that he wouldn't even be able to keep up with it.

"What's the matter?" asked the mouse. "I am so slow," sobbed Fat Puss, "that I can't even chase mice like all my friends do."

"I'm very glad about that," said the mouse. This made Fat Puss stop crying for a minute. "Why?" he asked. "Because we mice do not like being chased," replied the mouse.

"Really?" asked Fat Puss, who was very surprised at this.

"Yes," said the mouse, "we'd like cats a lot more if they didn't try to chase us."

"I never knew that," said Fat Puss,
cheering up a little. "I suppose it's a
good thing that I can't chase mice.
Could you be my friend?"

"Of course," said the mouse, "as long as you don't chase me. By the way, my name's Terence."

"My name's Fat Puss," said Fat Puss.

Terence and Fat Puss became very good friends and Fat Puss was very pleased that he had found a companion.

Terence took Fat Puss to meet his wife, Jessica, and his children, Robert and Charlotte.

Fat Puss spent many sunny afternoons playing with the mouse family.

When all the other cats saw what fun
Fat Puss was having they said, "Oh,
we wish we could play with the mice
like you, Fat Puss. But because we
chased them, they won't be friends
with us."

Fat Puss was very, very pleased that he had not done as the other cats had done because now he had made four new friends.

Fat Puss
in Summer

One warm summer day the sun was
shining brightly. Fat Puss felt so hot
and thirsty that he sat down for a rest
under a tree.

He saw all the other cats drinking
from the pond, stretching their long
necks so that they could reach the
water without falling in.

Fat Puss wanted a drink very much, so he tried to copy them. He bent down and stretched his neck out as far as he could, but he couldn't reach the water.

He stretched a bit more,

and a bit more,

until all of a sudden,

SPLOSH!!! He tumbled into the pond,
head first.

"What shall I do?" thought Fat Puss.
"I can't swim!"

Soon Fat Puss found that he didn't need to swim.

He was floating.

The other cats saw Fat Puss having fun floating in the water. So they tried to float too.

But they were so thin and bony that they couldn't float and they had to scramble quickly to the shore.

They climbed out looking wet and dripping. "We wish we could float in the pond like you, Fat Puss," they said.

Fat Puss was very glad that he could float in the pond. Now he could drink as much as he wanted to and have fun at the same time.

Fat Puss
Meets a Stranger

One day, Fat Puss went for a walk.

He came across a stream which he
had never seen before.

Fat Puss felt very hot, so he decided to jump in the water and float around for a while.

He enjoyed himself very much and he was glad that he had come across this new stream.

Suddenly, Fat Puss saw a brown,
furry creature swimming towards
him.

It raised its head and he saw that it had very large teeth.

"Oh dear," thought Fat Puss. "What shall I do? There is a brown, furry monster with big, sharp teeth coming towards me and it's going to eat me up!"

Fat Puss could not swim, but he tried to scramble away. The creature was coming nearer and nearer.

Fat Puss closed his eyes and waited for the attack . . .

"Hello," said a friendly voice.

Fat Puss slowly opened his eyes and realized that it was the brown creature who had spoken. "H-hello," returned Fat Puss nervously.

"Don't be afraid," said the creature, "I won't harm you."

"You mean you're not going to eat me up?" asked Fat Puss.

"Why, no, of course not," chuckled the creature. "I don't eat animals, I only eat plants."

Fat Puss felt very relieved.

"My name is Humphrey. I am a beaver," said the creature.

"I am Fat Puss," said Fat Puss.

"Now we know each other better, would you like to come for a swim with me?" asked Humphrey.

"I'm afraid I can't swim," replied Fat Puss sadly. "I can only float."

"I shall teach you how to swim, then!" exclaimed Humphrey.

"Thank you very much," said Fat Puss.

Humphrey taught Fat Puss how to
swim and they became very good
friends.

Fat Puss introduced Humphrey to Terence Mouse.

Fat Puss was very pleased to have found a new stream, learned to swim and to have made another nice new friend.

*Fat Puss
at Christmas*

One winter morning, Fat Puss went for a walk.

He discovered that everything was covered in something cold and white.

He didn't know what it was, so he went to ask Terence Mouse.

"Oh, that's snow," said Terence. "Don't be afraid of it, it's quite all right." Fat Puss decided to ignore the snow and do what he did every morning: roll down a few hills.

Fat Puss found a hill and began to
roll.

But, as he rolled, the snow stuck to
him and then more snow stuck to this
snow, and soon he looked like a large
snowball.

"Oh dear," thought Fat Puss. "I can't see where I'm going. What shall I do?"

BUMP! It was too late for Fat Puss to do anything.

He had bumped into a little fir tree
and it had knocked all the snow off
him. But the tree had fallen down.

Fat Puss didn't like to leave the tree lying on the hill because somebody else might trip over it. He did not know what to do with it, so he picked it up and took it to show Terence.

"It's a Christmas tree!" said Terence.
"We must decorate it, and then we
can sing carols around it on
Christmas Day."

"Oh, what a lovely idea!" exclaimed
Fat Puss.

Terence collected fir cones and old
leaves and conkers left over from
autumn.

Terence's children, Robert and
Charlotte, painted them bright
colours.

Terence's wife, Jessica, collected milk bottle tops that untidy people had dropped.

Then Fat Puss hung all the things on his tree until it looked gay and pretty.

Then, on Christmas Day, Fat Puss
and the Mouse family all had fun
singing carols around their own
Christmas tree. And Humphrey the
beaver joined them for tea.

The End.

Harriet Castor

FAT PUSS ON WHEELS

Illustrated by
Colin West

CONTENTS

CONTENTS

Fat Puss
on Wheels

One day, Fat Puss was
helping his friends, Robert and
Charlotte Mouse, to put some
rubbish on the rubbish dump.

"Look what I've found!"
Robert called out excitedly.

He held up a dirty piece of
metal with wheels on it.

"What is it?" asked Fat Puss.

"It's a roller-skate," said
Robert. "Can we play with it?"

"Well, I think we ought to
clean it first," said Fat Puss.

So Fat Puss, Robert and
Charlotte took the roller-skate
home and cleaned it until it was
bright and shiny. Then they had
great fun playing with it.

Robert and Charlotte sat on the roller-skate and Fat Puss pulled them along.

When Fat Puss got tired, they
pushed themselves along with
sticks instead.

"Why don't you try riding on it, Fat Puss?" they called.

"All right," said Fat Puss. He managed to sit on the roller-skate, but when Robert and Charlotte tried to pull him along, they just couldn't move him at all.

"Try pushing yourself along with a stick," suggested Charlotte.

But the stick snapped.

"Why don't you lie on your tummy and push yourself along with your paws?" said Robert.

But Fat Puss fell off.

"Perhaps it would be easier if you started at the top of a hill," said Charlotte.

"Yes," agreed Robert.

So Fat Puss took the
roller-skate to the top of a hill
and sat on it again. Sure
enough, he began to move.

"Isn't it wonderful?" cried the mice.

"Yes," shouted Fat Puss. The roller-skate started to go faster and faster. "But how do I stop?"

"Oh, dear," said Robert, "there's a river at the bottom of that hill."

Fat Puss hung on to the roller-skate and shut his eyes . . .

SPLOSH! He landed in the river.

Luckily, it wasn't very deep.

"Are you all right?" called the mice.

"Yes," replied Fat Puss. He tried to get up. "Except that I'm stuck in the mud!"

"Oh, no," said Robert. "What shall we do now?"

"I think we'd better get Mummy and Daddy," said Charlotte.

So the Mouse children left
Fat Puss sitting in the river, and
they ran to fetch Jessica and
Terence. Terence asked
Humphrey Beaver to come and
help too, and Jessica fetched a
piece of rope. Then they all
went back to Fat Puss.

"Don't worry, Fat Puss," said
Terence. "We'll get you out."
Humphrey jumped into the
river and tied one end of the
rope around Fat Puss's tummy.

Then all the mice pulled on the other end, while Humphrey pushed Fat Puss from behind.

"Pull! Pull!" shouted
Terence.

At last, with a squelch, Fat
Puss came out of the mud and

everyone fell over.

Fat Puss climbed on to the riverbank, covered in mud.

"I think you need a bath," laughed Terence.

"Yes," said Fat Puss. "Thank you for getting me out."

"But where's the roller-skate?" asked Robert and Charlotte.

"I'm afraid that got stuck in the mud too," said Fat Puss.

"And I think it ought to stay there," said Humphrey, "so that we don't have any more accidents."

Footballer
Fat Puss

One morning, Terence Mouse
visited Fat Puss. Terence looked
rather worried.

"What's the matter?" asked
Fat Puss.

"Well," said Terence. "We are supposed to be playing a football match tomorrow with the Rabbit family, but we need five players and there are only four of us. Would you play with us?"

FAT PUSS

"Of course," replied Fat Puss. Terence looked relieved. "But I've never played in a football match before."

"That doesn't matter," said Terence. "We've got all day to teach you."

So for the rest of the day, the Mouse family taught Fat Puss to play football. Robert and Charlotte helped him to practise running as fast as he could.

Jessica taught him how to
kick a ball.

And Terence explained
the rules of the game
to him. That evening Fat Puss
felt very tired and a little
nervous about the match.

The next morning, the Mouse
family went to see Fat Puss,
who was looking rather upset.

"Are you all right, Fat Puss?" asked Terence.

"No," sobbed Fat Puss. "Because of all that training yesterday, I feel stiff all over and I can hardly walk, let alone run."

"Oh, no," said Jessica. "What shall we do?"

"I'm so sorry that I've let everyone down," said Fat Puss.

"But you haven't!"
exclaimed Terence. "I've had
an idea. I don't know why we
didn't think of it before. Why
don't we let Fat Puss be the
goalkeeper? He's so big that he
won't have to move around
very much."

"That's a wonderful idea,"
said Jessica.

126

So the mice helped Fat Puss
to get to the football match,
and when it started, he stood in
the goal.

He found that he didn't need
to move at all because the ball
simply bounced off his tummy.

129

After the match all the mice hugged Fat Puss.

"You were so good," said Terence, "that we've decided to make you a permanent member of the team."

"Oh, thank you," said Fat Puss.

He was proud to be in the team and very happy that he hadn't let his friends down after all.

Flying Fat Puss

One sunny day, Fat Puss and his friends, the Mouse family, decided to go for a picnic. They all helped to pack the food in a basket and then they went to the park.

In the park, the Mouse
children played hide-and-seek.
Fat Puss joined in, although he
wasn't very good at it. First he
tried hiding behind a tree and

then he tried hiding under a pile
of leaves, but Robert and
Charlotte always found him
straight away.

While she was looking for somewhere to hide, Charlotte found a big bunch of shiny balloons tied to a tree. She untied one, and ran to show it to the others.

But suddenly she found that
she wasn't on the ground any
more. She was flying!

"Look at me!" she cried and then came back to earth with a little bump. "It's great fun!"

The other mice ran to get a
balloon and they found that
they could fly too. But Fat Puss
couldn't fly.

He held his balloon tightly,
and ran as fast as he could, but
he just couldn't get off the
ground.

"Never mind, Fat Puss," said
Terence. "I think it's time we
had our picnic."

"Oh, yes!" cried Robert and
Charlotte.

"But we should put the
balloons back first," said
Jessica.

"Oh, I'll do that," said Fat
Puss.

Everyone gave their balloons
to Fat Puss and he hurried over
to the tree.

Before he got there, he began to feel rather strange. His feet weren't on the ground any more. He was flying at last! He

went up and up until he was as
high as the treetops, and he
looked around at the wonderful
view.

As he drifted past a tree, he met Christine Crow. She was very surprised to see Fat Puss floating by.

Fat Puss was beginning to feel rather worried. "How shall I get down again?" he asked her.

"That is a problem," said Christine, "because if you just let go, you'll fall and hurt yourself." She thought for a moment. Then she had an idea.

"I know what to do," she said.

Christine popped one of the balloons with her beak.

Fat Puss sank down a little.
Then she popped another. Fat
Puss sank a little more.

Christine popped another,
and gradually Fat Puss sank all
the way back to the ground.

"Thank you, Christine," called Fat Puss.

The Mouse family were amazed that Fat Puss had flown so high.

"What does everything look like from up there?" asked Robert and Charlotte excitedly.

"Come on," said Terence. "Fat Puss will tell us all about it in a minute. But first we really must have our picnic!"

Fat Puss and the Baby Crows

One day, Christine Crow
came to see Fat Puss.

"I'm going to my sister's birthday party tonight," she said. "But I need someone to look after Katie, Lizzie and Kevin, my three babies, while I'm out. Would you mind looking after them for me, Fat Puss?"

"I'd love to!" said Fat Puss, feeling very proud that Christine had asked him.

So, that evening, Fat Puss
went to the tree where Christine
lived. Her nest was quite a long
way up.

"How will I get up there?" asked Fat Puss.

"Oh, dear, I didn't think of that," said Christine. "Aren't you very good at climbing trees?"

"Not really," replied Fat Puss.

"I'd better give you some help then," said Christine. "But I don't think I can manage it on my own. I know, I'll go and fetch Grandma Crow." And off she flew.

Very soon, Christine came
back with Grandma Crow.

"Now, Fat Puss," said
Christine, "Grandma and I will
help you. Don't worry."

But Fat Puss was worried.
He'd never climbed a tree
before.

First Christine and Grandma
Crow pulled him by his front
paws . . .

. . . and then they pushed him
up from behind.

Slowly, Fat Puss got from one branch to another, and before long he reached the nest.

"Well done!" chirped the baby birds.

Fat Puss could only just fit
into the nest, so Katie, Lizzie
and Kevin snuggled down on
his big, furry tummy.

Then Christine said
"Goodbye," and went off to the
party with Grandma Crow.

Fat Puss started to tell the
baby birds a bedtime story.
After a little while, it became
dark. Fat Puss started to feel
scared. He didn't like the dark.
Suddenly an owl hooted, and
Fat Puss almost fell out of the
nest with shock.

"What's the matter?" asked
the baby birds.

"I – I'm scared," said Fat
Puss.

"It's all right, Fat Puss," said
Lizzie. "It was only an owl."

But Fat Puss still looked very
worried. "I'm afraid of the
dark," he whispered.

"Never mind," said Katie.
"We'll sing to you to make you
feel better."

"Yes, that's a good idea!"
said Kevin.

So the three little birds
started to sing, and very soon
Fat Puss stopped being scared
and began to feel sleepy
instead.

When Christine Crow came home later that night, she found all four of them cuddled together, fast asleep.

Fat Puss
on Holiday

It was summer, and Fat Puss decided to go on holiday.

"Where shall I go?" he asked Terence Mouse.

"What about the seaside?" suggested Terence.

"That's a good idea," said Fat Puss. "But what could I do there?"

"Oh, lots of things," replied Terence. "You could build sandcastles, and collect shells, and swim in the sea."

"That sounds wonderful!" said Fat Puss.

So Fat Puss got out his suitcase, and the Mouse family helped him to pack. They put in Fat Puss's toothbrush, Fat Puss's pyjamas and Fat Puss's straw hat.

Then Fat Puss said goodbye
to the mice and to Humphrey
Beaver, and off he went to the
seaside.

Fat Puss spent all day
building a beautiful sandcastle,
collecting lots of interesting
shells and swimming in the
warm, blue sea.

The sun was shining brightly, and he felt very happy. "Oh, I love being on holiday," he said.

But the next day, Fat Puss
found that the sea had washed
his beautiful sandcastle away,
and where his pile of shells had
been he found only a rather
grumpy crab, who pinched his
paw.

The sky was cloudy and grey,
and when he swam in the sea, it
was very cold.

Fat Puss felt homesick. He didn't want to build sandcastles any more. He wanted to roll down hills like he did at home.

He didn't want to collect shells
any more. He wanted to talk to
the Mouse family. He didn't
want to swim in the sea any
more. He wanted to swim in the
river with Humphrey Beaver.

So Fat Puss put his toothbrush,
his pyjamas and his straw hat
back in his suitcase, and he set
off home.

As soon as Fat Puss got
home, he rolled down a hill.

Then he went to see the Mouse family. And then he went for a swim in the river with Humphrey Beaver.

"Did you enjoy going on holiday, Fat Puss?" asked Humphrey.

"Oh, yes, thank you," replied Fat Puss. "But I like coming home even more."

Also in Young Puffin

Rat Saturday

Margaret Nash

**"Go on, Joe, I dare you to go
to Teabag's."
"Right!" said Joe, suddenly feeling
brave. "I jolly well will go!"**

Does 'Old Teabag' really live in a damp
cellar with rats running up his legs? Joe
decides to find out. Imagine his surprise
when he meets two very friendly, very
tame pet rats! It's not long before Joe
and his friend Donna discover that tame
rats can be a lot of fun!

Also in Young Puffin

GEORGE SPEAKS

Dick King-Smith

Laura's baby brother George was four weeks old when it happened.

George looks like an ordinary baby, with his round red face and squashy nose. But Laura soon discovers that he's absolutely *extraordinary*, and everyone's life is turned upside down from the day George speaks!